Drug Use and Abuse

Perspectives on Physical Health

by **Bonnie Graves**

Consultant:
Nancy Mayer Gosz
Program Manager
Fairview Recovery Services, Adolescent Programs

LifeMatters
an imprint of Capstone Press
Mankato, Minnesota

LifeMatters Books are published by Capstone Press
PO Box 669 • 151 Good Counsel Drive • Mankato, Minnesota 56002
http://www.capstone-press.com

Printed in the United States of America

Library of Congress Cataloging-in-Publication Data
Graves, Bonnie B.
     Drug use and abuse / by Bonnie Graves.
          p.   cm.—(Perspectives on physical health)
     Includes bibliographical references and index.
     Summary: Discusses different kinds of illegal drugs, their effects on health and behavior, their use and the risks involved, options for treatment, and ways to stay drug-free.
     ISBN 0-7368-0416-1 (book)—ISBN 0-7368-0438-2 (series)
     1. Drug abuse—Juvenile literature. 2. Drugs of abuse—Juvenile literature.
     3. Teenagers—Drug use—Juvenile literature. 4. Teenagers—Drug use—Prevention—Juvenile literature. [1. Drugs. 2. Drug abuse.] I. Title. II. Series.
     HV5809.5 .G73 2000
     362.29—dc21

          99-049271
          CIP

Staff Credits
Rebecca Aldridge, editor; Adam Lazar, designer; Jodi Theisen, Heidi Schoof, photo researchers

Photo Credits
Cover: PNI/©StockByte
FPG International/©Barbara Peacock, 22
Index Stock Photography/9, 27, 57
International Stock/© Michael Agliolo Productions, 19; ©Jay Thomas, 59
©James L. Shaffer/41
Photo Network/©Esbin-Anderson, 16; Eric R. Berndt, 36
Photophile/©Alex Bartel, 15
Transparencies, Inc./©Billy E. Barnes, 53
Unicorn Stock Photos/©Steve Bourgeois, 32; Tom McCarthy, 46
Uniphoto/10, 38; ©Reins, 6; © Phil Cantor, 24; Llewellyn, 31, 49; Bob Daemmrich, 54

A 0 9 8 7 6 5 4 3 2 1

Table of Contents

Drugs contain chemicals that change the way the mind and body work.

Drugs can be used or misused. Drugs that are misused can be dangerous, addictive, and deadly.

There are six main types of drugs—depressants, stimulants, hallucinogens, narcotics, marijuana, and inhalants.

About 24 million people in the United States abuse drugs. About 5 million of those people are teens.

Chapter 1

Drugs—Just What Are They?

Luis was in ninth grade when he first sniffed paint thinner.

LUIS, AGE 15

His friend Carl had told him about it. "You feel buzzed. It's great," Carl had said. However, it wasn't so great for Luis. True, the first couple sniffs made him feel weird. Sure he felt different. But it wasn't great like he expected. He felt light-headed and confused. Then he got a headache and felt like he had to throw up.

Mind-Altering Chemicals

Most people don't think of paint thinner as a drug. Strictly speaking, it's not. Paint thinner is a solvent that makes other substances dissolve. It is used to thin paint or clean paintbrushes. However, it contains chemicals that act like a drug when inhaled.

A drug is any substance that changes the way the mind or body works. It may alter the way a person thinks, acts, or feels. Sniffing paint thinner made Luis feel light-headed. It gave him a headache and made him nauseous.

The brain is wired to work a certain way. Certain chemicals can change that wiring. Some chemicals can mess it up for a short time. Some mess up the wiring for a long time. Effects of these chemicals sometimes are irreversible or deadly.

"It was a nightmare," Hannah said. "I saw my roommate, Kim,

KIM, AGE 18

leave the party. She looked okay then. I knew she had been drinking. I got home late that night. Kim was already in bed. I didn't turn on the light because I didn't want to wake her up. The next morning I woke up at 11:00 A.M. Kim still hadn't stirred when I left for work. The cops were there when I returned to our apartment that afternoon. Kim was dead. She had died of a heroin overdose."

Drug Use and Abuse

Stages of addiction:

Experimentation: getting high to see what it's like

Routine use: needing more and more of the drug to get the same effect

Preoccupation: thinking about drugs more than anything else

Burnout: using any drug to get high

Use and Misuse

Of course not all drugs are bad for you. Many drugs help people. For example, aspirin can relieve headaches and muscle aches. Doctors prescribe many different drugs for many different problems. Any drug, however, can be dangerous if overused or misused. Some drugs have dangerous effects on some people but not on others. Some drugs are so potentially dangerous they are illegal.

> When Ron first started smoking marijuana, a couple puffs made him high. Soon it took a whole joint to get the same effect. It wasn't long before he was smoking a couple of joints a day to get the same buzz.
>
> **RON, AGE 16**

Tolerance

Often drug users develop a tolerance for a drug. They must take more and more of the drug to get the desired effects. Ron is an example of someone who has developed a tolerance for a drug.

Three common ways people take drugs include:

Ingesting: taking drugs orally by swallowing them

Inhaling: breathing in drugs through the nose or mouth

Injecting: releasing drugs directly into the bloodstream by using a needle

Addiction

Some drugs are addictive. That means the drug user gets used to having the drug. The person thinks that he or she must have the drug to survive. Drug users can become addicted both physically and psychologically, or mentally.

Physical addiction means the body gets used to having the drug. When it doesn't get the drug, the person experiences extreme physical discomfort. These withdrawal symptoms can range from nervousness to convulsions, or involuntary jerking movements. Withdrawal may even cause death.

Psychological addiction means the mind gets used to taking the drug. Having the drug becomes an important part of the user's life. The user feels as if life isn't good without the drug.

Six Main Types of Drugs

Many different drugs exist. However, there are six main types. These types are depressants, stimulants, hallucinogens, narcotics, marijuana, and inhalants. Examples of these drugs will be discussed in detail in chapters 2 and 3.

Depressants

Depressants are sometimes called downers. They are drugs that slow down the body. These drugs calm the user and cause sleep. They also impair judgment and are addictive. Examples of the most common depressants are alcohol and sedatives.

Stimulants

Some people may call stimulants uppers. These drugs have the opposite effect of depressants. They speed up the body. Stimulants act on the brain to give a short but strong burst of energy. All stimulants increase pulse rate and blood pressure. They also block feelings of hunger and fatigue. Caffeine, cocaine, crack, speed, and ice are examples of stimulants.

Hallucinogens

Hallucinogens also are called psychoactive drugs. Hallucinogens distort, or alter, the way a person perceives the world. They affect thoughts, feelings, emotions, and self-awareness. These drugs can cause a person to hallucinate, or see things that are not really there. Two examples of hallucinogens are LSD and PCP.

Narcotics

Narcotics are called opiates because they are opium-based drugs. These drugs relieve pain and cause sleep. All types of narcotics such as opium, morphine, and heroin are extremely addictive.

Marijuana

Marijuana also is known as cannabis. This drug blocks messages going to the brain. It alters how a person thinks, sees, feels, and hears.

Inhalants

Inhalants are another type of drug. Most inhalants are ordinary household products such as paint and aerosol spray. These products become drugs when they are sniffed or inhaled. Inhalants can be extremely dangerous.

Drugs and Teens

About 24 million people in the United States used illegal drugs in the past year. Sad to say, about 5 million of those people were teens. Some teens may just not know the facts about drugs. They may not know that using drugs risks losing their friends, health, future, and life.

Drug Use and Abuse

Myth: Everybody does drugs.

Fact: More than 86 percent of people ages 12 through 17 have never tried marijuana. More than 98 percent of kids in this same age range have never used cocaine. Only about half of 1 percent of kids in this age group have ever used crack.

Points to Consider

Why do you think some drugs are illegal?

Why aren't all drugs illegal?

What do you think it means to be addicted to a drug?

How do you think some people become drug abusers?

Four types of depressant drugs are alcohol, rohypnol, inhalants, and narcotics. Depressants slow down the brain and nervous system.

More people are addicted to alcohol than to any other drug. Alcohol can cause a person to lose control of thought and movement.

Rohypnol is a powerful sedative that can cause a person to pass out. Rohypnol is called the date rape drug.

Inhalants are drugs that users inhale or sniff. These drugs are extremely toxic and can cause brain damage, heart failure, and death.

Narcotics are a group of pain-relieving drugs. Heroin is the most abused narcotic. It is extremely addictive. Because tolerance develops so fast, users risk dying from an overdose.

Chapter 2

Alcohol, Rohypnol, Inhalants, and Narcotics

HUA, AGE 17

Hua sat in the auditorium as the ex-drug addict spoke. "Downers are addictive. At first they give you this great, relaxed feeling. Then, pow, before you know it, you're hooked. You've got to have your drug of choice, or else. It becomes the most important thing in your day and in your life. It takes control over you."

Hua was bored and slid farther down in her seat. She'd heard it all before. Alcohol, heroin, inhalants—what was the big deal, she wondered.

The liver needs about an hour to metabolize, or break down, the alcohol in one drink. During metabolization, the liver converts alcohol to water and carbon dioxide. Sweating, breathing, and urinating also help break down and use up the alcohol. If a person drinks more than ⅓ ounce of alcohol in an hour, he or she will usually feel its effects.

Depressants are a big deal because in addition to causing relaxation they also can cause addiction. If used the wrong way, depressant drugs can be dangerous or even deadly. Alcohol, rohypnol, inhalants, and narcotics are all examples of depressants.

Alcohol

More people are addicted to alcohol than to any other drug. About 18 million people in the United States are problem drinkers. Another 10 million are alcoholics, or people addicted to alcohol.

Alcohol affects every part of a person. People may drink alcohol for the immediate effects they expect it to have on them. For example, they may think drinking can stimulate them or make them less self-conscious. However, alcohol slows down the brain and nervous system because it is a depressant. People under the influence of alcohol cannot think or act quickly. Their vision is distorted. Their balance and judgment are off. Alcohol affects mood, speech, and coordination.

One of the most serious risks of drinking is loss of control. The drinker can lose control of speech, movement, and thought. This puts drinkers at risk for out-of-control behavior that can lead to serious injury or even death. Drinkers become more at risk than nondrinkers to act violently or irresponsibly.

MARVIN, AGE 17

Marvin was at a party that one of the guys on the basketball team was throwing. Marvin began the evening with a couple of beers. Later on he had some mixed drinks as well. Then, Marvin bragged about being able to drink vodka straight from the bottle. A crowd gathered around Marvin and cheered him on as he chugged the liquor. Just as he emptied the bottle, Marvin passed out. Marvin died of alcohol poisoning.

Alcohol is not only a drug but also a poison. A person can die if too much alcohol enters the body too quickly. Mixing alcohol with other drugs can be lethal, or deadly, too. Alcohol and drugs increase the effects of each other, and that increases danger to the user.

Karin met Sean at a party.
She'd never seen him before.

They had a few drinks together. Then Sean asked Karin if he could take her home. On the way to her apartment, Karin felt very sleepy. The next thing she remembered was waking up on the floor of her apartment. She had no clothes on. She had a horrible headache. She couldn't recall anything about the night before. Sean was gone. She didn't know where he lived. She didn't even know his last name. Karin knew one thing, though. She had been raped, or forced to have sex.

Rohypnol

What Karin didn't realize was that Sean had slipped rohypnol into her drink. Rohypnol is a small, white pill that dissolves quickly. Rohypnol, like alcohol, is a depressant. It is a type of sedative that is sold legally in Mexico and South America. These tablets come in packaging much like cold medicine. However, this drug is illegal in the United States.

Rohypnol often is called the date rape drug. On the street, rohypnol tablets are called roofies. Abusers slip this drug into their victim's drink. The drug makes a person feel sleepy, and eventually the person passes out. Rohypnol can wipe out a person's memory for six to eight hours. Victims who are raped have no memory of the attack.

Drug Use and Abuse

People can try to protect themselves from drugs such as roofies. At parties or during dates, people should watch what they drink. Also, they should avoid taking drinks from someone they don't trust or know well.

DID YOU KNOW?

Inhalants

Like alcohol and other sedatives, inhalants are depressants. Most of the time the effects of inhalants are similar to those of alcohol. That is, they cause slurred speech and lack of coordination. Users may feel light-headed. They also may feel giddy, or dizzy and excited. The effects of inhalants usually last less than an hour.

Inhalants come in three categories. These are solvents, gases, and nitrites. Solvents include such products as gasoline and paint. Gases are found in common items such as cooking spray or spray paint. Nitrites are chemicals that are found in room deodorizers.

All inhalants are extremely toxic. They can destroy brain cells on contact. They also can cause an immediate overdose. When this happens, a person gets more of the drug than his or her body can handle. This occurs with inhalants because sniffing delivers a quick, powerful shot of toxic chemicals straight from the nose to the brain. Another danger comes from sniffing aerosol spray inhalants. These inhalants can coat the air cells of the lungs with paint and other gunk and cause suffocation.

Street names for rohypnol and heroin:

Rohypnol: roofies, LaRocha, ropies, roachies, wolfies, ruffies

Heroin: chiva, horse, hammer, junk, smack, brown sugar

Narcotics

Heroin is one of a group of drugs known as narcotics. These drugs relieve pain. The two types of narcotics are opiates and synthetics. Opiates such as heroin and morphine come from an herb called the opium poppy. Synthetics are drugs such as Darvon® and Demerol® that are created in labs. Heroin accounts for 90 percent of the opiate abuse in the United States. It is sold as a brown or white powder or as a dark, sticky resin. Heroin can be smoked, sniffed, or injected.

Heroin is a powerful sedative that slows down the body. At first, heroin causes users to feel a short rush of pleasure. After that they feel relaxed and have no pain. The pupils of heroin users contract until they are tiny. Users may become sleepy, dizzy, or nauseous. Also, their breathing may slow.

Heroin users quickly develop a tolerance to the drug. A heroin addict's life revolves around getting and using the drug because it is highly addictive. People addicted to heroin must have the drug or they suffer withdrawal. Some of the physical withdrawal symptoms of heroin are chills and vomiting, or throwing up. Another sympton is diarrhea, a condition in which normally solid waste becomes runny and frequent.

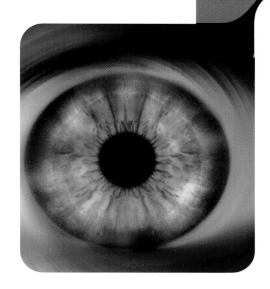

Using heroin involves many risks. Because tolerance develops so fast, users risk dying from an overdose. An overdose can cause the person to choke on his or her own vomit. Overdosing also can cause convulsions or coma—a state of deep unconsciousness. Another risk exists because the quality of heroin is unpredictable. Users never know what is in the heroin they are buying.

Points to Consider

What makes all depressants potentially dangerous?

Why do you think alcohol is the most abused drug?

Why are roofies sometimes called the date rape drug?

If someone asked you to try an inhalant, how would you respond?

Because marijuana affects memory, thought, and motor skills, it puts users at risk for unsafe behavior. Marijuana also lowers sex hormone levels. This can cause a delay in puberty, or sexual development.

Amphetamines are stimulants that speed up the body's systems. They increase heartbeat and blood pressure and decrease appetite.

Cocaine and crack also are stimulants that give a brief high followed by a painful low. Both drugs are extremely addictive and dangerous.

Hallucinogens mess up the senses. They alter the way a person perceives the world. This change puts the user at risk for serious injury and death.

Chapter **3**

Marijuana, Amphetamines, Cocaine and Crack, and Hallucinogens

"You've been smoking pot for some time haven't you, Lamont?" Dr. Sanchez said.

Lamont shrugged. He wasn't going to admit to anything. Whether or not he smoked pot was his business.

"Well, you need to know this," Dr. Sanchez said. "Marijuana affects the hormone testosterone. Hormones are chemicals in the body that determine how you grow and develop sexually. You're not as physically developed as most other boys your age are. It could be because of THC. That's the main chemical in marijuana."

Marijuana

Marijuana, or cannabis, comes from the leaves and flowers of the hemp plant. Marijuana is usually rolled into cigarettes or stuck into hollowed-out cigars called blunts. Sometimes it's smoked in water pipes called bongs. Marijuana contains a drug known as tetrahydrocannabinol, or THC.

Many teens aren't aware of the risks of smoking pot. Marijuana use affects memory, motor skills, thoughts, and emotions. It reduces the ability to think and move. It also can make people careless about what they do or say. This puts them at risk for unsafe behavior. Heavy marijuana use can cause a teen to lose interest in school, family, and friends.

Marijuana affects the body, too. It causes an increase in appetite that can lead to weight gain. It increases heart rate. Marijuana causes bloodshot eyes and dry mouth and throat. It also lowers the level of sex hormones. This can affect a teen's sexual development and physical growth. Also, for males, marijuana use as a teen may lead to impotence later in life. Men who are impotent are unable to engage in sexual activity.

Street names for drugs:

Amphetamines: crank, meth, crystal, speed, ice, uppers, ups, black beauties, pep pills, copilots, bumblebees, hearts, footballs, glass

LSD: acid, white lightning, domes, flats, frogs, California sunshine, mellow yellow, tabs, wedges

PCP: angel dust, ozone, wack, rocket fuel, peace pill, elephant tranquilizers, dust

Amphetamines

Amphetamines are stimulants that speed up the body's systems. Users of these drugs report a sense of well-being, high energy, cleverness, and power. The effects are similar to cocaine but last longer—from four to six hours. Amphetamines can be taken orally, injected, smoked, or snorted. Amphetamines raise heartbeat and blood pressure and decrease appetite. Weight loss due to this decrease in appetite can lead to malnourishment. This is because the person does not get the vitamins and minerals needed for good health. Then the person may not be able to fight off disease.

Methamphetamine, or speed, has stronger effects than other amphetamines. Speed comes in a pill form. It also comes in a powder form that is snorted or injected. Both ways of taking the powder are painful.

The crystallized form of methamphetamine is known as ice. This form of the drug can be smoked and is more powerful than speed. Ice is highly addictive and toxic. Users quickly develop a tolerance to this drug. Both speed and ice cause increased activity and insomnia, or inability to sleep. They also can cause a person to become anxious and confused.

SAFFRON, AGE 18

Saffron first started smoking ice at an all-night dance party, or rave. She got addicted quickly. After a rave, she would smoke ice for three days. She kept smoking because she didn't want to crash from the high. Crashing depressed her. All Saffron could do when she stopped smoking was sleep.

Saffron was a talented painter, but she soon lost interest in her art. She had very little energy. In fact, it was hard to feel pleasure in anything anymore. She smoked ice to try to get that pleasure back.

Cocaine and Crack

Cocaine and crack come from the leaves of the South American coca plant. Cocaine is a white powder that can be snorted or injected. Crack is cocaine processed into tiny rocks that a user smokes. Crack is stronger and more addictive than cocaine.

Like an amphetamine, cocaine is a stimulant. It speeds up the brain and body and increases heart rate and blood pressure. Cocaine and crack cocaine give a brief and temporary burst of pleasure and energy. After this high, the user feels low and edgy and craves more of the drug. Both cocaine and crack cocaine are extremely addictive.

Effects of drugs:

Marijuana: dry mouth and throat, bloodshot eyes, increased heart rate and appetite, impaired memory, reduced ability to perform tasks, and paranoia, or distrust and suspicion of others

LSD and PCP: hallucinations, depression, confusion, tremors, anxiety, lack of coordination, strange or violent behavior, flashbacks, and poor perception of time and distance

Cocaine and crack: increased blood pressure, heart and breathing rate, and body temperature; heart attack, stroke, and brain seizure; violent, erratic, or paranoid behavior; confusion, anxiety, and depression

"Get them off me!" Josh yelled.

"Get what off you?" Terrell asked.

JOSH, AGE 17

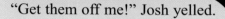

"The bugs! They're crawling all over me!" Josh said in a panic.

"It's the crack, man. Nothing's on you," Terrell said.

Crack and cocaine put users at risk for violent, unpredictable behavior. They put users at risk for hallucinations, too. That means the user sees or hears things that are not really there. One common hallucination is a feeling that insects are crawling over the drug user's skin. Cocaine and crack have played a part in many drownings, car crashes, falls, and burns. Some people have committed suicide, or killed themselves, after taking cocaine or crack. Even first-time users are at risk for a fatal seizure or heart attack. Even some extremely fit athletes have died of heart attacks caused by cocaine.

People addicted to cocaine and crack lose interest in life. Things that used to give pleasure such as food, friends, and family don't anymore. Researchers believe this happens because cocaine permanently changes the way the brain works. It reduces the brain's ability to produce dopamine. This is a substance the brain releases whenever a person has a pleasurable experience.

Underground chemists create designer drugs. These drugs have similar effects to other illegal drugs but have a slightly different chemical makeup. Dealers sell these drugs because they do not have to be smuggled in from another country. In many cases, designer drugs are stronger and more dangerous than the original drug. LSD and ecstasy are both examples of designer drugs.

Hallucinogens

Hallucinogens are psychoactive drugs. Some of the drugs in this group are LSD, phencyclidine (PCP), and ecstasy. The drug ecstasy is a speed-based psychedelic. Other drugs like it include mescaline, peyote, and psilocybin, or magic mushrooms.

As a group, hallucinogens don't look or act the same as each other. However, they all cause some of the same effects. These effects include changes in mood, thought, and behavior. These drugs all induce hallucinations.

Hallucinogens mess up the senses. Some people on these drugs may "see" sounds and "hear" colors. A person's sense of direction, distance, and time also get mixed up. The effects of these drugs usually last between 4 and 12 hours. However, they can last up to 24 hours. Other physical effects of these drugs include increased heart rate and blood pressure, lack of muscle control, and tremors. Incoherent, or unclear, speech is another physical effect of hallucinogens.

One risk of hallucinogens is the unpredictable and violent behavior they can cause. This behavior can lead to serious injury and death. Another risk of taking these drugs is self-inflicted, or self-made, injuries due to decreased awareness of touch and pain.

LSD users risk overdosing. That is because LSD produces tolerance in the user. This tolerance means the user needs higher and higher doses to get the same effect. Users rarely know exactly what is in the drug, so these higher doses increase the risk for overdose. This could result in convulsions, coma, heart and lung failure, or even death.

Points to Consider

Why is marijuana a particularly dangerous drug for teens?

What are some of the effects stimulants have on the body?

There's a saying "What goes up, must come down." How might this relate to the powerful stimulants speed, ice, cocaine, and crack?

How would you react if someone you knew started hallucinating because he or she had taken drugs?

Chapter Overview

Teens usually take drugs because of a strong need. The person's need usually is combined with a lack of information about the drug.

Teens sometimes start taking drugs to relieve stress and emotional pain.

Some teens take drugs to rebel against authority. Some teens take drugs to fit in with their peers. Teens sometimes try drugs out of curiosity or desire for a new experience.

The negative consequences of illegal drugs outweigh any perceived benefits.

Chapter **4**

Why Do Some Teens Abuse Drugs?

People use and abuse drugs for many different reasons. Usually, however, a strong need is involved. The person takes the drug to satisfy the need he or she feels. The need might be to relieve stress or to feel like part of a group. It might be to satisfy curiosity or to rebel. Often the person's need is combined with a lack of information about the drug.

"Using drugs didn't help with my problems. They added more."
—Shiquita, age 13

"There are a few druggies at our school. Most kids find better ways to get high, though. They get into sports or music or whatever."
—Nathan, age 15

"Yeah, sure. I've thought about trying drugs, but I've never done it. I just don't think it's worth the risk. I don't want to become one of those horror stories. I don't want to end up in the hospital emergency room or spending all my money on drugs."—Giselle, age 16

"Want to know my theory? People who take drugs just don't feel that good about themselves. They think drugs are the answer for whatever is hurting inside them."—Kurt, age 17

A Need to Feel Better

Teens may use drugs to try to make themselves feel better. The teen years are full of pressure. Teens are expected to do and learn a lot. Sometimes teens think their problems are unsolvable. These pressures can cause stress and depression. Some teens turn to drugs. They think drugs can get rid of their emotional pain.

ERIC, AGE 14

Eric thinks his parents treat him like a baby. Every day, they add a new rule to their list. Eric is sick of it. He is tired of them always telling him what to do. Eric wishes he could be more like the guys that hang out at the video arcade. They don't seem to have a worry in the world. Eric knows they smoke pot. Sometimes he can smell it. If only the guys would offer him a joint. He'd take it. Wouldn't that make his parents furious?

A Need to Rebel

Taking drugs is a way for some teens to rebel. By taking drugs they are saying, "I can do what I want. I can make my own decisions."

Melinda was thrilled. Someone from her new school invited her **MELINDA, AGE 17** to a party. However, when Melinda got to the party, everyone was drinking wine coolers and beer. None of her friends at her last school drank. Melinda had never touched booze before. She didn't want to drink, but she didn't want to be labeled a loser, either.

A Need to Be Liked and to Fit In

Having friends is a big need for everyone. Teens especially feel pressure to fit in. Unfortunately, this peer pressure is one of the most natural parts of growing up. Some teens may think drugs can help them feel less uptight. Some teens may think drugs will make them funnier or more relaxed. A teen may hang out with a group that uses drugs. That teen may feel the need to do drugs as well.

Everyone feels peer pressure. However, the less sure people are about themselves, the more likely they are to cave in to peer pressure.

"I've got some ice," Natalie whispered. "You want to smoke some?"

"What's it like?" Felicia asked.

"An awesome high. The best," Natalie said.

"Sure. I'll try it," Felicia said.

A Need for a New Experience

Some teens might try drugs because they are curious. They may have heard stories about how drugs can make a person feel and act. They may want to find out for themselves. Some teens are risk takers and rebels. They may try drugs just to have a new experience. However, they may not consider the consequences.

Know the Consequences

Taking drugs always comes with consequences. It is important for teens to be aware of these consequences. This knowledge can help teens decide the best way to satisfy the needs that they feel.

"One of the reasons I got hooked on heroin was that first great high. I kept taking the drug, trying to get there again. You're always chasing after that first high, but you never catch it. You keep on trying. Soon, all you think about is that next hit. That's when you know the drug is chasing you."—recovering heroin addict

"I was always looking for a way to feel better. It never occurred to me that I could do that without drugs."
—recovering cocaine addict

Points to Consider

Do you think people who take drugs to help with stress solve their problem in the long run? Why or why not?

What are some ways that drugs are used to rebel?

How would you handle peer pressure to take drugs?

Would you be tempted to try a drug just for the thrill of a new experience? Why or why not? What are some new, exciting experiences you could try that do not involve drugs?

Taking any drug involves risks.

Drugs can cause people to lose control physically and emotionally.

Teens who take drugs risk losing friends who do not use drugs.

Health risks from drug use vary from weight gain to brain damage.

People who do drugs put their present, future, and life at stake.

Chapter 5

Risks of Using Drugs

Taking any drug involves risk. Even drugs that are legal carry risks. For example, some people are allergic to aspirin. Some people avoid caffeine because of the negative effects it has on them. A person never knows exactly how his or her body will react to any drug.

The risks of illegal drugs are even greater. For one, the drugs are illegal (including alcohol for people under age 21). That means a user risks being fined, jailed, or both.

Also, illegal drugs that are sold have no quality control. That means users never know what exactly is in the drugs they are taking. They also do not know the amount they are getting. Heroin could be mixed with chalk or laundry detergent. Sometimes less powerful drugs are mixed with more powerful drugs. This is done so dealers can make more money. Therefore, drug users face the risk of unexpected or deadly reactions.

HARD LESSONS

"I took LSD because I wanted a new thrill. The first couple of trips were awesome. Then came the third trip. It felt like my skin was being ripped off. I panicked because I couldn't do anything to stop it. When the drug wore off, I was wet. My T-shirt was soaked with sweat and I had peed. It was gross. I still have flashbacks about that trip."—Justin, age 18

"People told me the risks of using cocaine. But I didn't listen. I thought, 'That can't happen to me.' What people couldn't tell me was what it felt like to almost die. I also spent six months in jail for stealing stuff to support my habit. Those lessons I had to learn for myself. I wish I had known."—Tamara, age 16

Drug Use and Abuse

Even one hit of crack or cocaine can be fatal.

Cocaine is an expensive habit. Many users turn to prostitution and other crimes to pay for their habit.

Risk of Losing Control

Drugs screw up the brain. A person who takes a drug is letting chemicals have their way with his or her mind. These chemicals can change the way a person thinks, sees, acts, or feels. The person is no longer in the driver's seat. Drugs can cause a person to lose control of:

Judgment and reasoning

Reaction time

Coordination

Speech

Thought and memory

Behavior

Risk of Losing Friends

Kristie had hung out with Jen and Maja during junior high. In

KRISTIE, AGE 14

ninth grade, she met Diane, who was a junior. Kristie admired her. Diane smoked pot. Soon Kristie was smoking, too. She started skipping classes and her grades dropped. Jen and Maja quit hanging around with Kristie.

One day, Diane just dropped out of Kristie's life. Diane didn't come back to school. Kristie never found out where Diane went. It was a huge blow for Kristie. She felt totally alone. With Diane gone, she no longer had any friends.

Drug users risk losing the people they care about most. Most teens do not use drugs. A few, like Diane, do. Kristie was impressed by Diane. However, teens who use drugs often are unpredictable and unreliable. Teens who get involved with drugs risk losing friends who do not use drugs.

Some ways that death can occur with inhalant use:

Asphyxiation—happens when solvent gases limit available oxygen and cause breathing to stop

Suffocation—can happen when users inhale with bags

Choking on vomit

Sudden sniffing death syndrome—causes the heart to stop

Health Risks

Drug use takes its toll on the body. It robs a person of his or her health. Each drug has its own set of health risks. These risks may include:

- Weight loss or gain

- Red eyes and constant runny nose

- Loss of coordination or balance

- Sleep problems

- Skin problems

- Heart and nervous system damage

- Brain damage

Trevor was 12 when he started
drinking alcohol. At age 14, he

TREVOR, AGE 17

started smoking pot and then crack cocaine. At 16, he became
a heroin addict. Trevor's whole life revolved around getting
and taking drugs. Nothing else mattered. He spent all the
money he made at the car wash on drugs. When that wasn't
enough, he started stealing. Trevor had no present and no
future, only his drug habit. It ruled and ruined his life.

Risk to Your Present and Future

Drugs took control of Trevor and his life. Trevor lost his teen
years to addiction. Drugs robbed him of his money. They robbed
him of having fun and discovering who he was. They also kept
him from developing relationships and learning skills that would
help him lead a happy life. Teen years are critical for developing
problem-solving skills. Instead of discovering positive ways to
solve his problems, Trevor turned to drugs. They didn't solve his
problems. Instead, they added to them.

Risking Your Life

People who take drugs risk death. Drugs can cause fatal strokes
or heart attacks. Taking drugs can lead to fatal accidents because
they impair judgment and coordination. People who take drugs
are at risk for fatal falls, drownings, and car accidents. Drug
users also can become severely depressed and hopeless. Drugs
can trap users in a vicious cycle that may lead to suicide.
Accidental drug overdose also can result in death.

Everyone Loses

Everyone loses when it comes to using or abusing illegal drugs. Users can lose their self-respect and relationships. They lose their health and sometimes their lives. Nonabusers lose, too. Sometimes innocent people are killed or lose loved ones because of drug abuse. Friends and family members of drug users suffer. Society suffers because of drug-related crime and health-care costs.

Points to Consider

What are some of the risks of taking drugs?

What do you think is the greatest risk of taking drugs? Explain.

If you choose to take drugs, what are your reasons for doing so? If you choose not to take drugs, what are your reasons for not doing so?

Do you think that teens who take drugs know about the risks? Why or why not?

Denial is usually what keeps drug abusers from getting help. It is one of the symptoms of addiction.

Drug addiction is a treatable disorder. Treatment programs usually fall into three categories—outpatient care, inpatient hospitalization, and residential programs.

Counseling and support groups are part of all treatment programs.

Methods for treating drug abusers are different, but the goals are the same. One goal is to help the abuser stay off drugs. The other is to help the abuser learn the skills needed to stay drug-free.

Any successful drug-abuse treatment includes the family as well as the abuser.

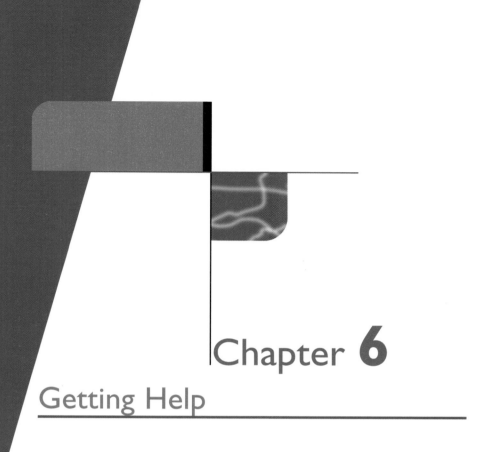

Chapter **6**

Getting Help

Admitting a Problem Exists

A drug addict usually has a difficult time admitting that a problem exists. This difficulty is what keeps the abuser from getting help. Drug addiction can happen to anyone. Answering some tough questions can help someone who thinks he or she might be addicted to drugs. The National Council on Alcoholism and Drug Dependence (NCADD) suggests the questions on the following page.

Are You At Risk?

Do you use drugs to build self-confidence?	YES	NO
Do you ever take drugs right after you have a problem at home or school?	YES	NO
Have you missed school because of drugs?	YES	NO
Does it bother you if someone accuses you of abusing drugs?	YES	NO
Have you started hanging out with a drug-using crowd?	YES	NO
Do you feel sad or depressed after using drugs?	YES	NO
Have you been in trouble for using drugs?	YES	NO
Have you lost friends since you started using drugs?	YES	NO
Do you feel a sense of power when you use drugs?	YES	NO
Do you ever wake up and not know what happened the night before?	YES	NO
Do you think you have a drug problem?	YES	NO

Three "yes" answers to any of the previous questions indicate a risk for drug addiction. Five "yes" answers indicate that immediate professional help is needed.

Denial is a powerful tool for defense. It protects a person from an unpleasant truth. Most drug addicts won't admit they're addicted because they're in denial. The truth is too painful for them to face.

GINA, AGE 19

Gina seemed like a normal teen. She did well in school. She had plenty of friends. She was a talented oboe player. However, Gina also was a rebel. She liked being smart, but she didn't like being labeled "teacher's pet." She dyed her hair black. She pierced her ears, nose, and eyebrow. She started talking back to the adults in her life. It gave her a feeling of power.

However, deep inside, Gina felt something was wrong. She often felt depressed and anxious. She didn't know how to get rid of those feelings. When the vet prescribed tranquilizers for her dog, Gina thought she'd try some herself. Then Gina tried marijuana. She used marijuana and alcohol all through high school.

Gina met Rolf at college. He introduced Gina to heroin. At first, heroin took away Gina's anxiety. It gave her a rush of pleasure. Heroin seemed like a miracle drug.

Gina kept taking heroin, always chasing that first great experience. It never came, though. "I'm doing what I want. I'm in control," Gina told herself. One night she overdosed. A friend had to call 9-1-1.

Treatment

Drug addiction is a treatable disorder. In treatment programs, people learn to live happily without drugs. They learn to change their behavior. Often they take medication as part of their treatment. After treatment, people can go on to lead normal, productive lives. The goals of all drug-abuse treatment are the same. They are to stop the person's drug use and to improve the person's ability to function. Another goal is to minimize any complications of drug use.

Treatment programs usually fall into three categories. These categories are outpatient care, inpatient hospitalization, and residential programs.

Outpatient Care

Some people with drug problems can be treated as outpatients. That means they don't have to stay in a hospital. Instead, they go to a clinic at regularly scheduled time periods. Their treatment includes individual counseling, peer-group counseling, and family therapy. Outpatient drug-free treatment does not include use of medication to help the person recover.

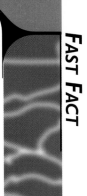
Inpatient Hospitalization

A hospital stay is one recommendation for serious drug abusers. A hospital stay usually lasts about 10 to 14 days. Patients get a physical and psychological exam. They are stabilized medically and emotionally. Some people go through mental and physical withdrawal. Treatment includes individual, group, and family counseling.

Residential Programs

Another option for serious drug abusers is a residential treatment center, or therapeutic community (TC). Longtime abusers who have not had success with other approaches usually attend these centers. In treatment centers, patients have time and space to look realistically at their life. In this respectful, supportive environment, they can work to make some life changes. Some treatment centers are just for teens. The teens live and attend school there. They also spend 25 to 30 hours per week in individual, group, and family therapy.

A stay at either a hospital or a residential program safely gets the user out of a dangerous situation. It also removes the abuser from his or her drug contacts.

"I began a treatment program when I was 15. The counselors helped me, but recovery couldn't have happened without hashing things out with other kids like me. We'd dig up a lot of stuff and talk about it. Those group sessions really hurt sometimes. Still, they made me feel I wasn't alone. I wasn't the only one with problems."—Steve, age 18

"I hated those group sessions at first. I didn't want to talk about that crap they got into. I don't know how it happened, but finally I opened up. I learned how to ask for help. That's when things started to get better for me."—Maria, age 15

There is no best method for treating drug abuse. In all types of treatment, patients need to unlearn old patterns of thought and behavior. These are the patterns that have kept them on drugs. Treatment goals also are the same. One goal is to help the abuser stay off drugs. The other is to help the abuser learn the skills needed to stay that way. Recovery consists of six steps. To recover, a drug user needs to:

Admit a problem exists

Get off and stay off drugs

Accept the support of others

Develop nondrug friendships and interests

Develop the coping skills needed to deal with work and relationships

Have self-respect and look forward eagerly and confidently to each day

"You don't know what it's like to have a drug addict in the family. You can't have a normal life, whatever normal means."

ALLY, AGE 14

What Family and Friends Can Do

Everyone in a drug abuser's life is affected, especially family. Effective treatment programs include family counseling. Family members need appropriate help to recover as well. Al-Anon and Alateen are two organizations that help friends and family members of alcoholics and other drug abusers. Their numbers are listed at the back of this book.

Family and friends alone can't give the help drug abusers need. They need the help of people trained to treat the disorder. However, it is important for family and friends of drug abusers to accept that the abuser has a disorder. They also should learn to stop rescuing the abuser from his or her mistakes. Another important step for family and friends to take is to seek information on drug abuse. It's important to remember that drug abuse is a treatable disorder. Abusers can recover and lead productive lives.

Points to Consider

Why do you think many drug abusers have a hard time admitting they have a drug problem?

What are some other ways a drug user could cope with a problem instead of taking drugs?

Why is it important for family members to be involved in a drug abuser's recovery?

Change is a key aspect to look for if you suspect someone of using drugs. This change could be in appearance, behavior, or both.

You can help a friend with a drug problem by voicing your concern and being a good listener. You can offer to help, to get information, and to get help for yourself.

If you think you have a drug problem, you can learn the facts about drugs. You also can accept that you have a problem and take action.

Drug abuse can be prevented.

Chapter **7**

What You Can Do

SHANNON, AGE 15

"Do you think Shannon has been acting weird lately?" Nisha asked.

"What do you mean?" Cicero replied.

"Well, she seems so moody. And she's never home when I call," Nisha said.

"Yeah. You're right. I ran into her in the hall yesterday. Her eyes were all bloodshot. She looked at me with this blank stare. I wonder what's going on."

"My friends and I knew Troy was doing drugs, but we didn't want to bust him. So we didn't tell. Now we wish we would have. At his funeral his parents asked us, 'Did you know?'"—Paki, age 15

"I didn't want Celia to get mad at me, so I didn't tell her parents she was taking heroin. I told a counselor instead. She called Celia's parents. Celia's in a treatment program now. She still doesn't know how her parents found out, and we're still friends."—Anna, age 17

How can you tell if someone has a drug problem? The key is to look for change. This change could be in the person's physical appearance. It also could be a change in the person's behavior or personality. It could be a combination of changes in appearance, behavior, and personality. Here are some of the symptoms to watch for:

Physical symptoms:

Change in appetite and unexplained weight gain or loss

Sleep disturbance or unusual laziness

Red and watery eyes, change in usual pupil size, blank stare

Cold and sweaty palms, shaky hands, feet, or head

Puffy face, paleness, or blushing

Excessive talking or extreme hyperactivity, or restlessness

Runny nose, hacking cough

Needle marks on lower arm, leg, or bottom of feet

Nausea or vomiting

Excessive sweating

Behavioral/psychological symptoms:

Change in overall attitude or personality with no other identifiable cause

Change in friends or hangouts, sudden avoidance of old friends

Drop in school grades or work performance, misses or is late for school or work

Difficulty paying attention, forgetfulness

Lack of motivation, energy, self-esteem, and concern

Oversensitivity or resentfulness, has temper tantrums

Moodiness, irritability, or nervousness

Silliness or giddiness

Paranoia

Excessive need for privacy

Secretive or suspicious behavior

Chronic, or continued, dishonesty

Unexplained need for money, stealing

If You Suspect a Friend Has a Drug Problem

If you suspect a friend has a drug problem, you can voice your concern. However, nagging or scolding the person won't do any good. Your friend will probably deny the problem anyway.

It is important not to accuse the person of being an alcoholic or drug addict. Instead, pick a time when your friend isn't under the influence of drugs. Have another friend with you. There is safety and support in numbers. Then tell the suspected user what you've noticed and why you're worried. Talk about how it makes you feel to see him or her high.

It is best not to try to help your friend on your own until you have talked with an adult you trust. This could be a counselor, teacher, doctor, nurse, parent, or spiritual leader. You don't have to mention your friend by name. Talking with this trusted adult can help you figure out the best course to take.

Your friend needs to talk with someone he or she can trust, so be willing to listen. He or she needs support and understanding. Find out where help is available. Sources to get you started are listed at the back of this book. You can offer to go with your friend to get help. If you offer this support, be prepared to follow through.

The Starfish Foundation is a group of high school and college students. They talk with teens about the importance of breaking the code of silence about drugs. They tell teens how to inform parents of drug abusers in a confidential way. That way no one will know it was the teen who told.

Drug users often do not want help. Naturally, it is hard to help someone in this case. However, the National Council on Alcoholism and Drug Dependence (NCADD) can provide assistance. This organization operates a National Intervention Network. This network helps to plan, rehearse, and conduct an intervention. During an intervention, specially trained people meet with the suspected drug abuser. This process can bring change to a drug user's life. You can call NCADD and ask for help. The number is listed at the back of this book.

You also may want to get help for yourself, so you can better understand your friend's problem. If so, you can contact Alateen or Nar-Anon Family Group. These numbers are listed at the back of this book, too. These groups can give you tips on how to deal with your friend. They can help you deal with your own feelings, too.

It is important to get all the information you can about drug abuse. The more information you know, the more you can help your friend. Remember, however, it's up to your friend to get help. It's not your responsibility to make that happen. All you can do is show how much you care.

How to say "no":

"I'm in training."

"I'm allergic."

"There's something important I've got to do in a little while. I won't be able to do it if I'm high."

"I'm taking a prescription that reacts badly with it."

"You do what you want. I'd rather make up my own mind."

"I'm not interested."

"Sorry. I have to drive."

"I made a deal with myself not to do drugs."

"No, thanks."

Jill started out smoking a few joints on the weekends. Normally she was uptight at parties. Pot relaxed her. She felt she had more fun when she smoked. Soon, however, a few joints didn't do the job anymore. Jill started to wonder if maybe she had a drug problem.

JILL, AGE 16

If You Abuse Drugs

Maybe you suspect you have a drug problem. This is a good time to take action. Asking yourself the questions on page 44 may determine if you need help. Remember, if you have a drug addiction, the hardest part is accepting your problem.

It also is important to look for better ways to solve your problems. Talking with a doctor, nurse, or counselor may be helpful. You may want to join Alcoholics Anonymous or Narcotics Anonymous. Doing these things will make many people, including yourself, happy.

"Drugs are around. I know that sooner or later I'll end up at a party with kids doing drugs. Will I think about how crack could fry my brain? Or will I try it because everybody else is?"

PAUL, AGE 15

To Keep Yourself From Taking Drugs

You can do several things to keep from taking drugs. It is a good idea to keep active and busy in school and the community. Another good idea is to do fun stuff with friends that doesn't involve drugs. It also is important to find at least one adult you can talk with about your problems.

Learning the facts can help teens say "no" to drugs. However, pressure situations may still be hard to face. You could say "no" by:

Giving a reason. For example, someone might say, "Try some pot. You'll have a better time." You could say, "Smoking makes me sick. I'm already having a good time."

Having something else to do. "No, thanks. I'm going to dance."

Being prepared for different kinds of pressure. If the pressure seems threatening, you can just walk away.

Making it simple. There's no need to explain if you don't want to. Just say, "No, thanks." If that doesn't work, say it stronger.

Tips for staying drug free:

"Find an adult who can help you get through the rough times."
—Shawna, age 16

"Set some goals. Think about what you want to do next week, next summer, and next year. These are things you want to do that make you feel good about yourself, things that make you happy."—Grant, age 18

"Stick with a group of friends who don't use drugs."—Renell, age 13

"Feed your spirit with good things such as music or books. Take a walk in the woods. After all, you are what you see, hear, and think about."
—Jodi, age 18

Another solution may be to avoid pressure situations. You may choose not to go to a party if you know there's going to be alcohol or drugs. If you think there may be alcohol or drugs at a party but still want to go, you might try this. Make a decision in advance not to drink or do drugs. Then, if someone asks you, you will have an answer prepared.

To Keep Your Peers From Using Drugs

There are a couple of things you can do to keep your peers from taking drugs. One is to be a good role model. If you choose to say "no" to drugs, most likely your friends will, too.

Another thing you can do is join Students Against Destructive Decisions (SADD). One of the things SADD does is promote drug-free parties. SADD has chapters in every state. The address and Internet site for SADD are listed at the back of the book.

Points to Consider

What would you do if you noticed a friend showed several of the signs for drug abuse?

Who are three trusted adults you could talk with about drugs or other problems?

What are some of the things drug users can do to help themselves?

What do you think is the best way to prevent drug abuse?

Glossary

addictive (uh-DIK-tiv)—habit-forming

drug (DRUHG)—a substance that changes the way the brain and body work

hallucination (huh-loo-suh-NAY-shuhn)—something seen, heard, or sensed that doesn't really exist

hormone (HOR-mohn)—chemical in the human body that determines how people grow and develop sexually; hormones control body function.

insomnia (in-SOM-nee-uh)—inability to sleep

intervention (in-tur-VEN-shuhn)—an action taken to change a situation

lethal (LEE-thuhl)—deadly

medication (med-uh-KAY-shuhn)—a substance used to treat an illness or injury

psychoactive (sye-koh-AK-tiv)—affecting the mind or behavior

sedative (SED-uh-tiv)—a drug that causes a person to feel calm or relaxed

symptom (SIMP-tuhm)—sign or evidence of a disease or disorder

synthetic (sin-THET-ik)—artificial; made by humans rather than nature.

therapy (THER-uh-pee)—any treatment meant to improve a person's health or well-being

tolerance (TOL-ur-uhnss)—the mind and body needing more and more of a drug to get the same effect

withdrawal (with-DRAW-uhl)—the period following the discontinued use of a habit-forming drug; withdrawal often is marked by uncomfortable physical and psychological symptoms.

For More Information

Bayer, Linda N. *Crack and Cocaine.* Philadelphia, PA: Chelsea House, 1999.

Graves, Bonnie. *Alcohol Use and Abuse.* Mankato, MN: Capstone Press, 2000.

Hyde, Margaret O. *Know About Drugs.* 4th ed. New York: Walker and Co., 1995.

McLaughlin, Miriam Smith, and Sandy Peyser Hzouri. *Addiction: The "High" That Brings You Down.* Springfield, NJ: Enslow, 1997.

Sprung, Barbara, and Suzanne J. Murdico. *Drug Abuse.* Austin, TX: Raintree Steck-Vaughn, 1998.

Useful Addresses and Internet Sites

American Council for Drug Education
(ACDE)
164 West 74th Street
New York, NY 10023
1-800-488-DRUG
www.ACDE.org

Canadian Centre on Substance Abuse
75 Albert Street, Suite 300
Ottawa, ON K1P 5E7
CANADA
www.ccsa.ca

Nar-Anon Family Group Headquarters, Inc.
PO Box 2562
Palos Verdes Peninsula, CA 90274
www.syix.com/mleahey/United/index.htm

Narcotics Anonymous (United States)
PO Box 9999
Van Nuys, CA 91409

National Council on Alcoholism and Drug
Dependence (NCADD)
12 West 21 Street
New York, NY 10012
1-800-NCA-CALL
www.ncadd.org

Students Against Destructive Decisions
(SADD)
PO Box 800
Marlboro, MA 01752
www.saddonline.com

Do It Now Foundation Online
www.doitnow.org
Offers access to online publications about
drugs as well as to games that test and teach
about drugs

Drug Education and Awareness for Life
(DEAL)
www.deal.org/english/html/main
Includes online newsletters, real-life stories,
and library

Freevibe
www.Freevibe.com
Provides information for teens about drugs,
tips on drug-free activities, and the opportunity
to share personal stories

Al-Anon/Alateen
1-800-344-2666 (United States)
1-800-443-4525 (Canada)
www.al-anon.alateen.org

Index

Index continued

jail, 35, 36
judgment, 9, 14, 37, 40

LSD, 9, 23, 25, 26–27, 36

marijuana, 7, 8, 10, 11, 21–22, 25, 30, 38, 40, 45, 56
memory, 16, 22, 25, 37
methadone, 47
methamphetamine, 23
mood, 6, 10, 14, 26, 51, 53
morphine, 9
myths, 11

narcotics, 8, 18–19. *See also* heroin; morphine; opium
National Council on Alcoholism and Drug Dependence (NCADD), 43, 55
National Intervention Network, 55
"no," saying, 56–58

opium, 9, 18
outpatient care, 46
overdose, 6, 17, 19, 27, 40, 45

paint and paint thinner, 5–6, 10, 17
paranoia, 25, 53
passing out, 15, 16
PCP, 9, 23, 25, 26
peer pressure, 30, 31, 57–58
problem-solving skills, developing, 40

rape, 16
reaction time, 14, 22, 37
rebelling, 29, 30, 32, 45
residential programs, 47

rohypnol, 16, 17
role models, 58

seizures, 25
sexual development, 21–22
sleep problems, 8, 9, 16, 18, 23, 24, 39, 52
speech, 14–15, 17, 26, 37
speed, 9, 23
Starfish Foundation, 55
stealing, 36, 40, 53
stimulants, 8, 9. *See also* amphetamines; caffeine; cocaine; crack; ice; speed
stress, 29, 30
Students Against Destructive Decisions (SADD), 58
suffocation, 17, 39
suicide, 40

THC (tetrahydrocannabinol), 21–22
thought, 6, 9, 15, 22, 26, 37, 48
throwing up, 5, 6, 18, 19, 39
tolerance, 7, 18–19, 23, 27
tranquilizers, 45
treatment, 46–48, 52

using drugs, methods of
    ingesting, 8, 23
    inhaling, 5, 6, 8, 10, 18, 23, 24, 38, 40
    injecting, 8, 18, 23, 24

vision, 10, 14

weight loss and gain, 9, 22, 23, 39
withdrawal symptoms, 8, 18, 47